THE GLORY BUS

The Kingdom to the Capitol Adventures of

Written by Sean Feucht & Liafaith

Copyright ©2024 by Sean Feucht Published by Sean Feucht Created by Lia Faith Fischer ISBN:979-8-9893944-2-5 All rights reserved. No parts of this publication may be reproduced, stored in a retrieval system, or transmitted in any form or by any means, electronic, mechanical, photocopying, recording, or otherwise, without the prior written permission of the copyright owner.

This book is sold subject to the condition that it shall not, by way of trade or otherwise, be lent, resold, hired out, or otherwise circulated without the publisher's prior consent in any form of binding or cover other than that in which it is published and without a similar condition including this condition being imposed on the subsequent purchaser. Under no circumstances may any part of this book be photocopied for resale. Illustrated by Acamy Schleikorn. Printed in the United States of America.

God loves America so much, and we are so excited to be on this amazing Jesus Journey with you!

So, come on! Let's go on our Kingdom to the Capitol Adventures!

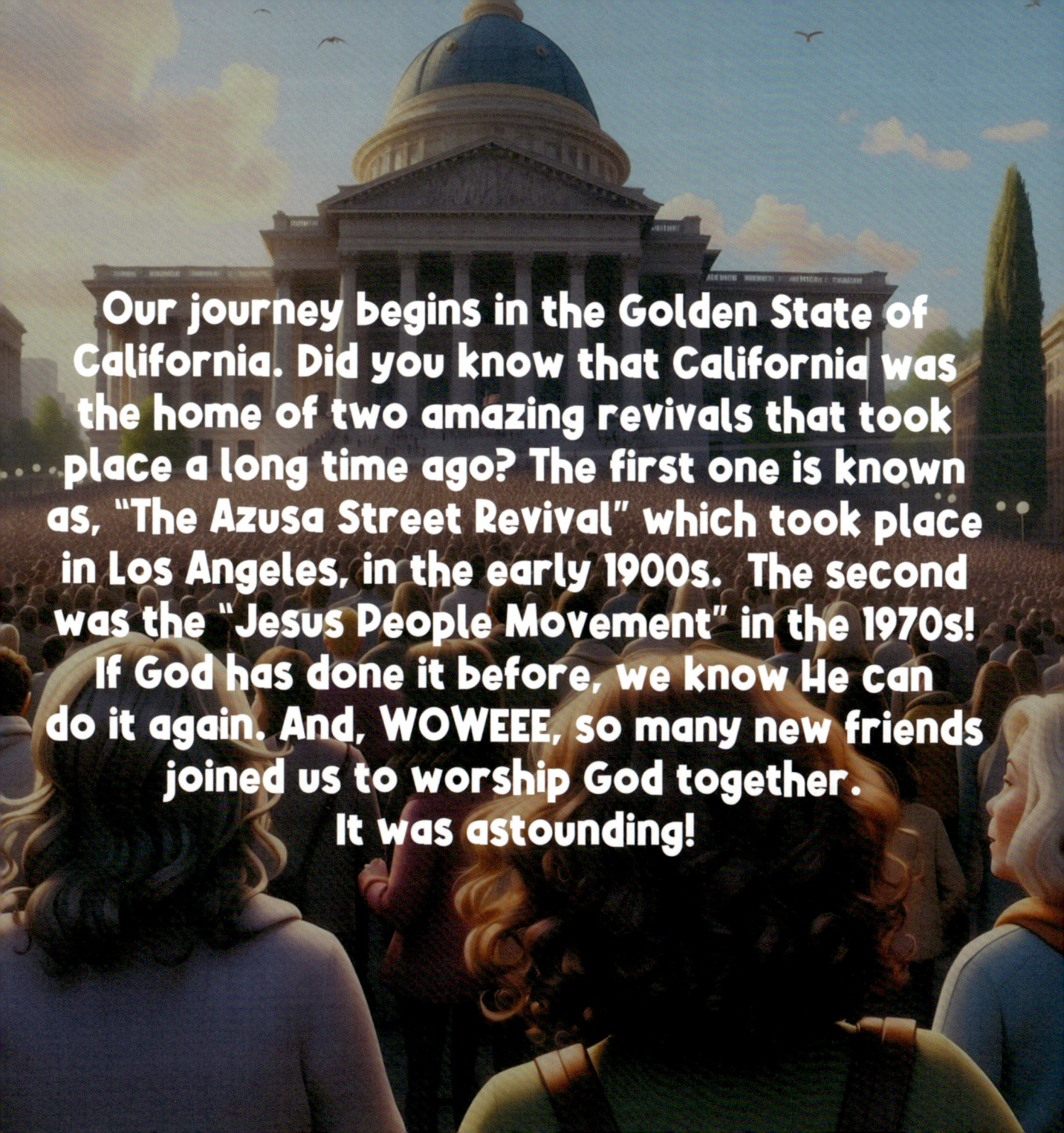

Our journey begins in the Golden State of California. Did you know that California was the home of two amazing revivals that took place a long time ago? The first one is known as, "The Azusa Street Revival" which took place in Los Angeles, in the early 1900s. The second was the "Jesus People Movement" in the 1970s! If God has done it before, we know He can do it again. And, WOWEEE, so many new friends joined us to worship God together. It was astounding!

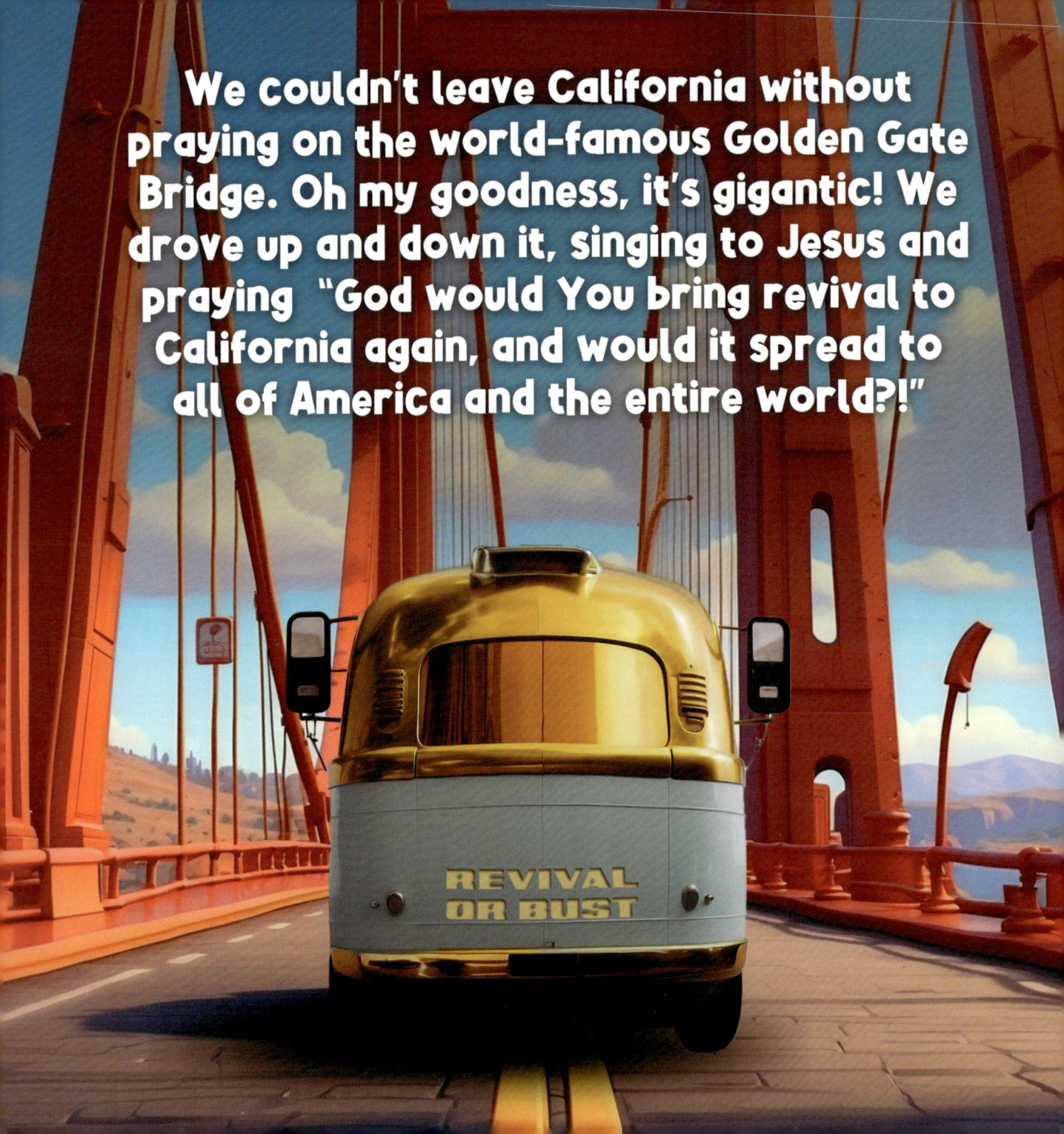

We couldn't leave California without praying on the world-famous Golden Gate Bridge. Oh my goodness, it's gigantic! We drove up and down it, singing to Jesus and praying "God would You bring revival to California again, and would it spread to all of America and the entire world?!"

Next, we get to go to a part of America called the Pacific Northwest. I drove through so many amazing mountains and forests- it was so beautiful. We worshipped Jesus with thousands and thousands of people in Boise, Idaho, then in Olympia, Washington, and even more in Salem, Oregon!

What an amazing trip! Until...
Watch out! Oh, no! I got a flat tire!

Praise the Lord, we had just made it to Montana! The new friends we met there were so kind to me. They rolled me into a rodeo ring, so I could rest and get some new tires! Of course, we had to worship at the rodeo!

Yee-haw, thank the Lord, and let's keep going!

We get to worship Jesus everywhere we go: past Yellowstone National Park in Wyoming, through Salt Lake City, Utah, and Carson City, Nevada. We even got to worship on the Hoover Dam! Seeing all that water in the desert reminded me of a Bible verse:

"I am doing something new! Now you will grow like a new plant. I will even make a road in the desert, and rivers will flow through the dry land." - Isaiah 43:19

Did you know that God can do impossible things? When we put our trust in Him, we will see Him do amazing things!

We've got to keep going! We have a lot of ground to cover if we're going to make it to the Nation's Capitol!

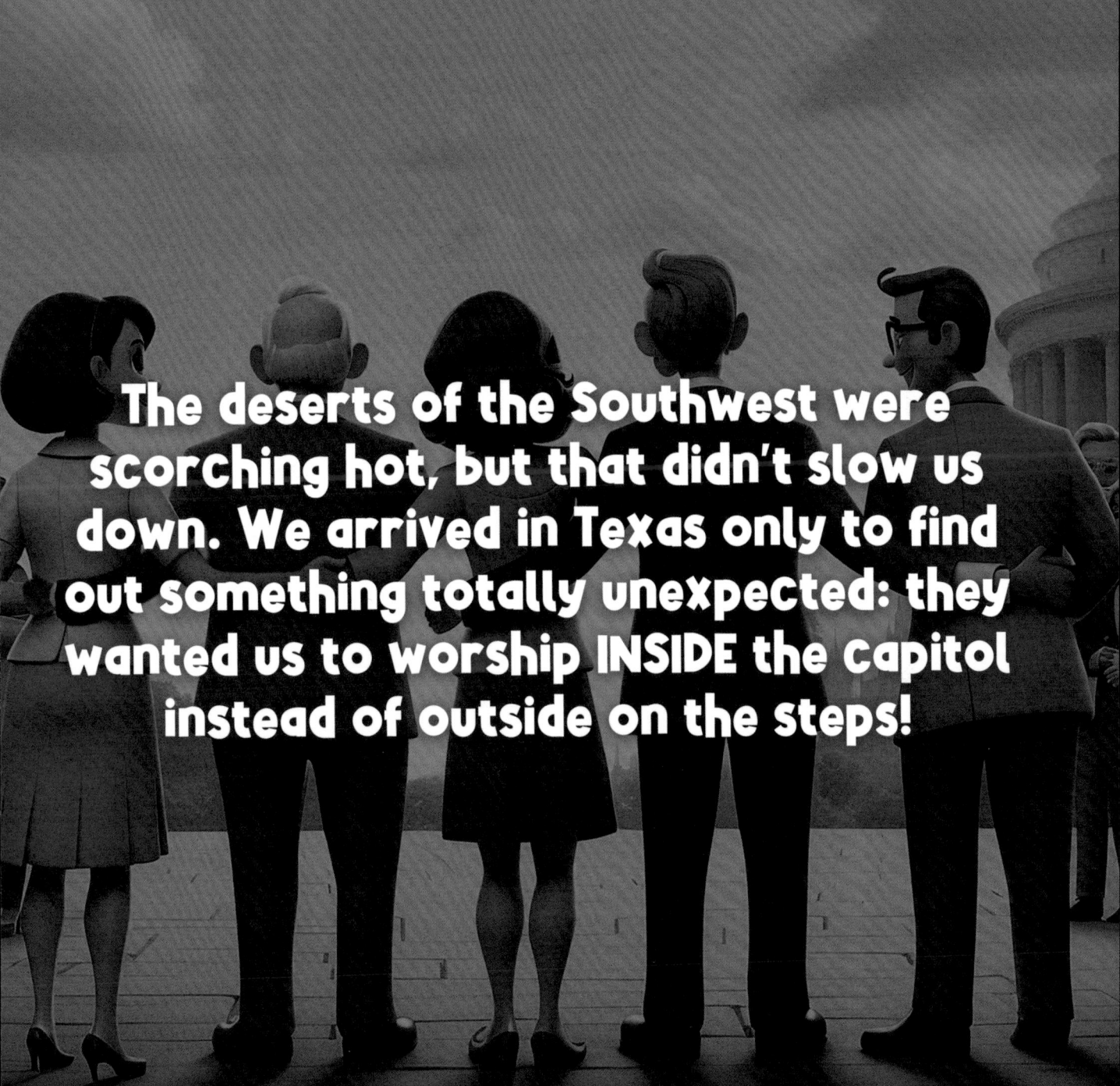

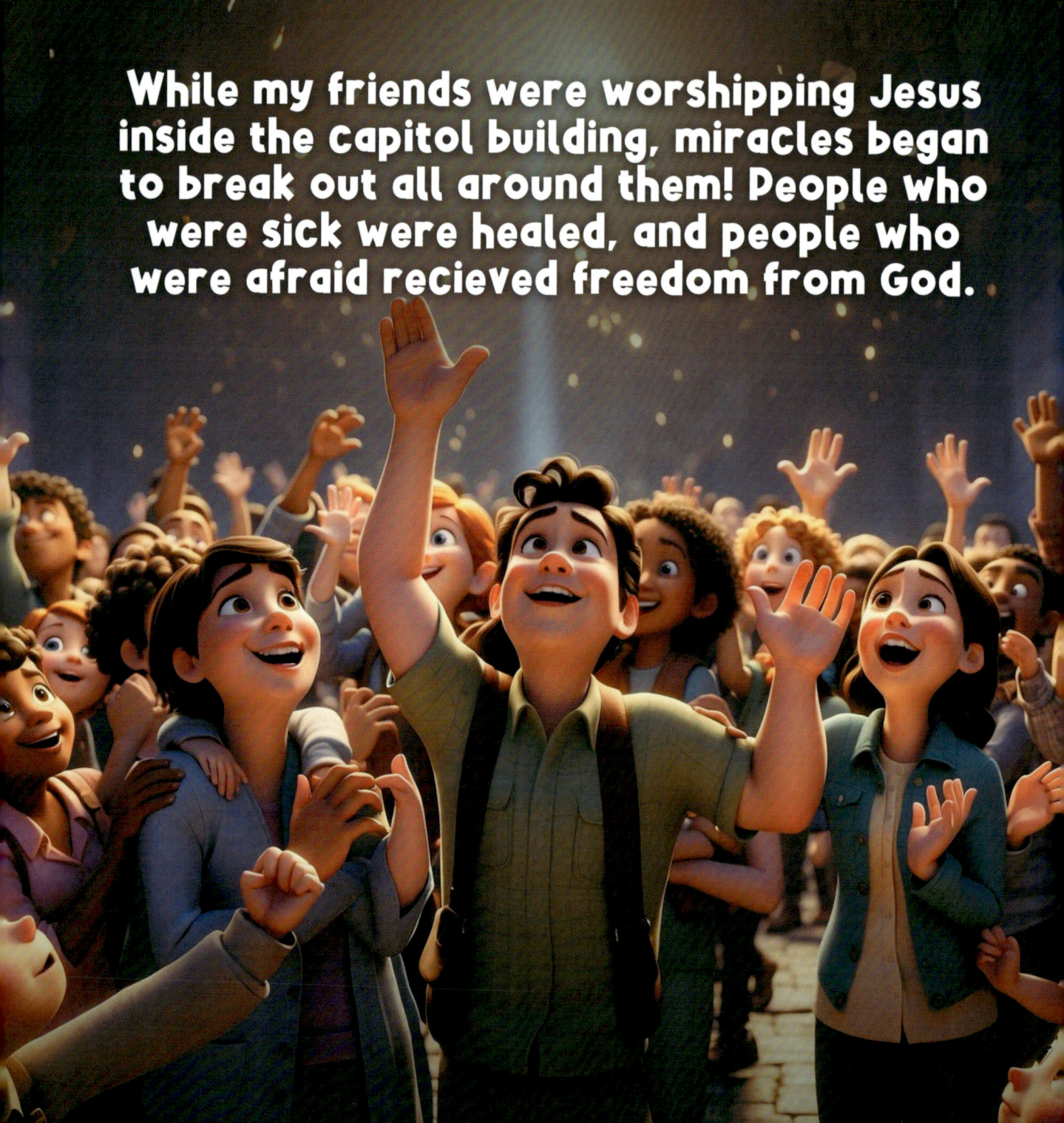

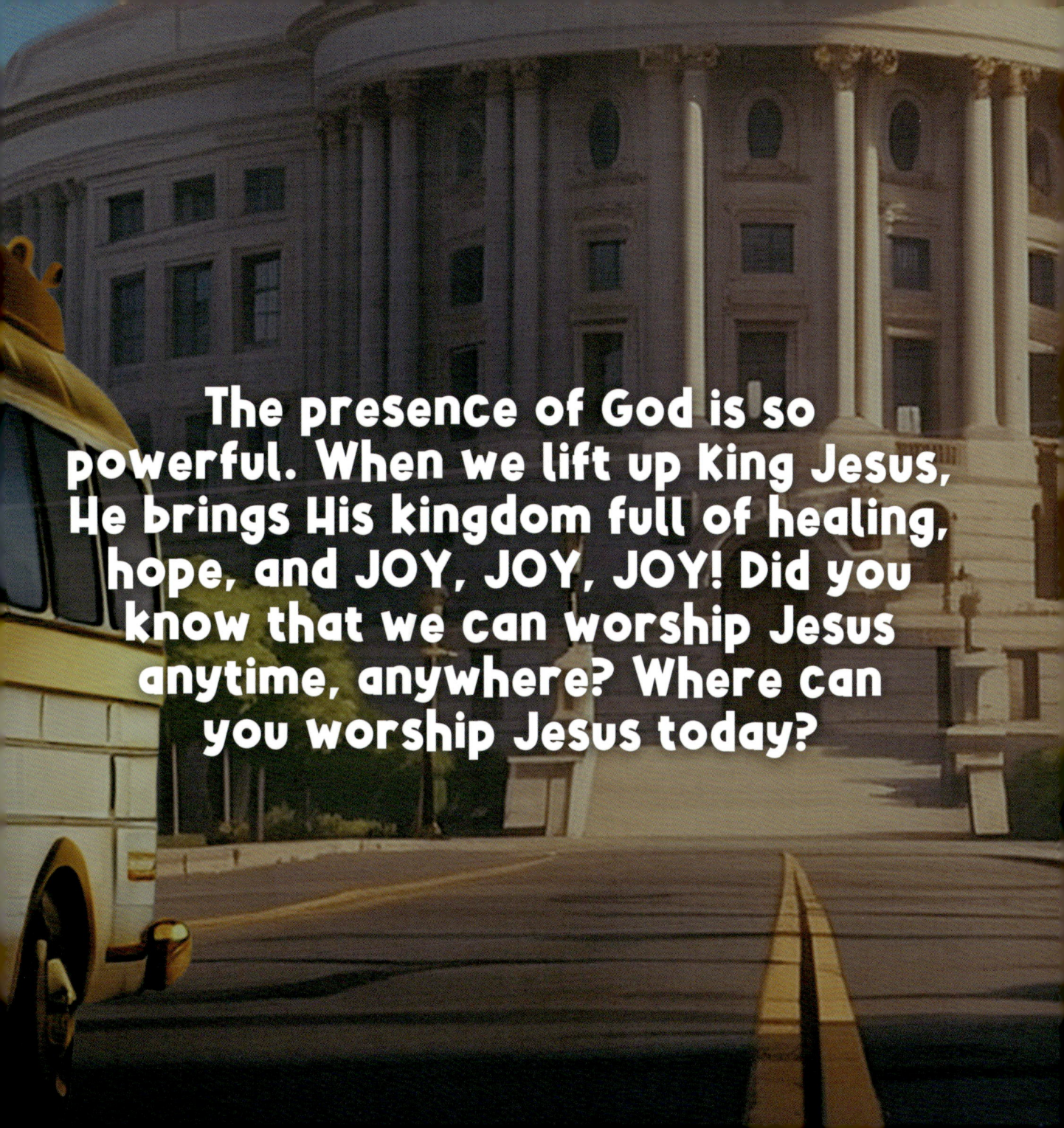

The presence of God is so powerful. When we lift up King Jesus, He brings His kingdom full of healing, hope, and JOY, JOY, JOY! Did you know that we can worship Jesus anytime, anywhere? Where can you worship Jesus today?

Worshipping Jesus in Texas was a great way to kick off our time in the South! We bounced all around the Bible Belt, praying, worshipping, and sharing the love of God everywhere we went. When we were done, we made a special stop in Selma, Alabama.

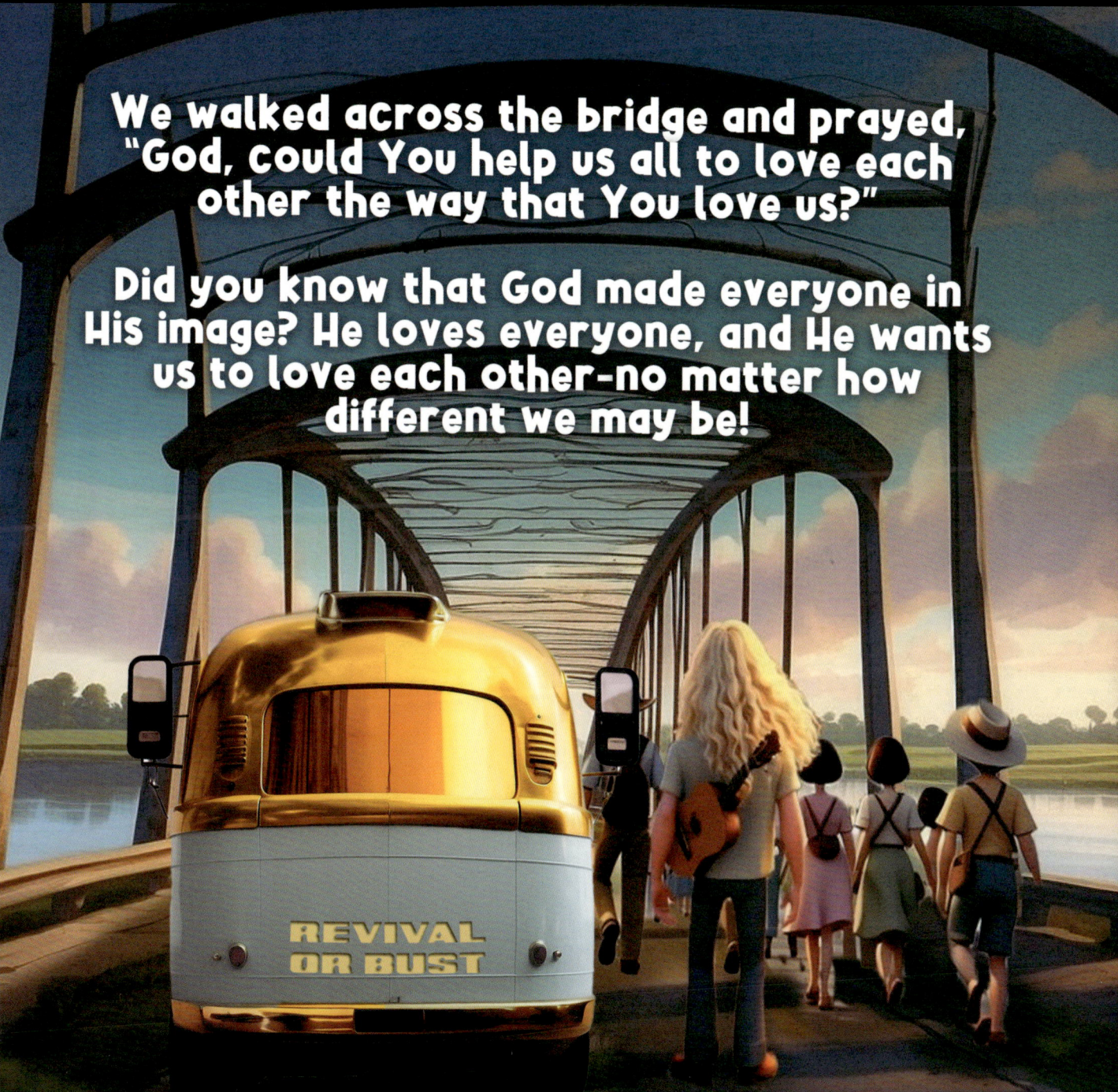

We walked across the bridge and prayed, "God, could You help us all to love each other the way that You love us?"

Did you know that God made everyone in His image? He loves everyone, and He wants us to love each other—no matter how different we may be!

While we loved spending time in the South, there were still many more miles to go. Off to the American Heartland: the Midwest! From the Gateway Arch in St. Louis, to the cornfields of Indiana, to the big giant bean in Chicago, all the way to Mount Rushmore in South Dakota, God led us every step of the way.

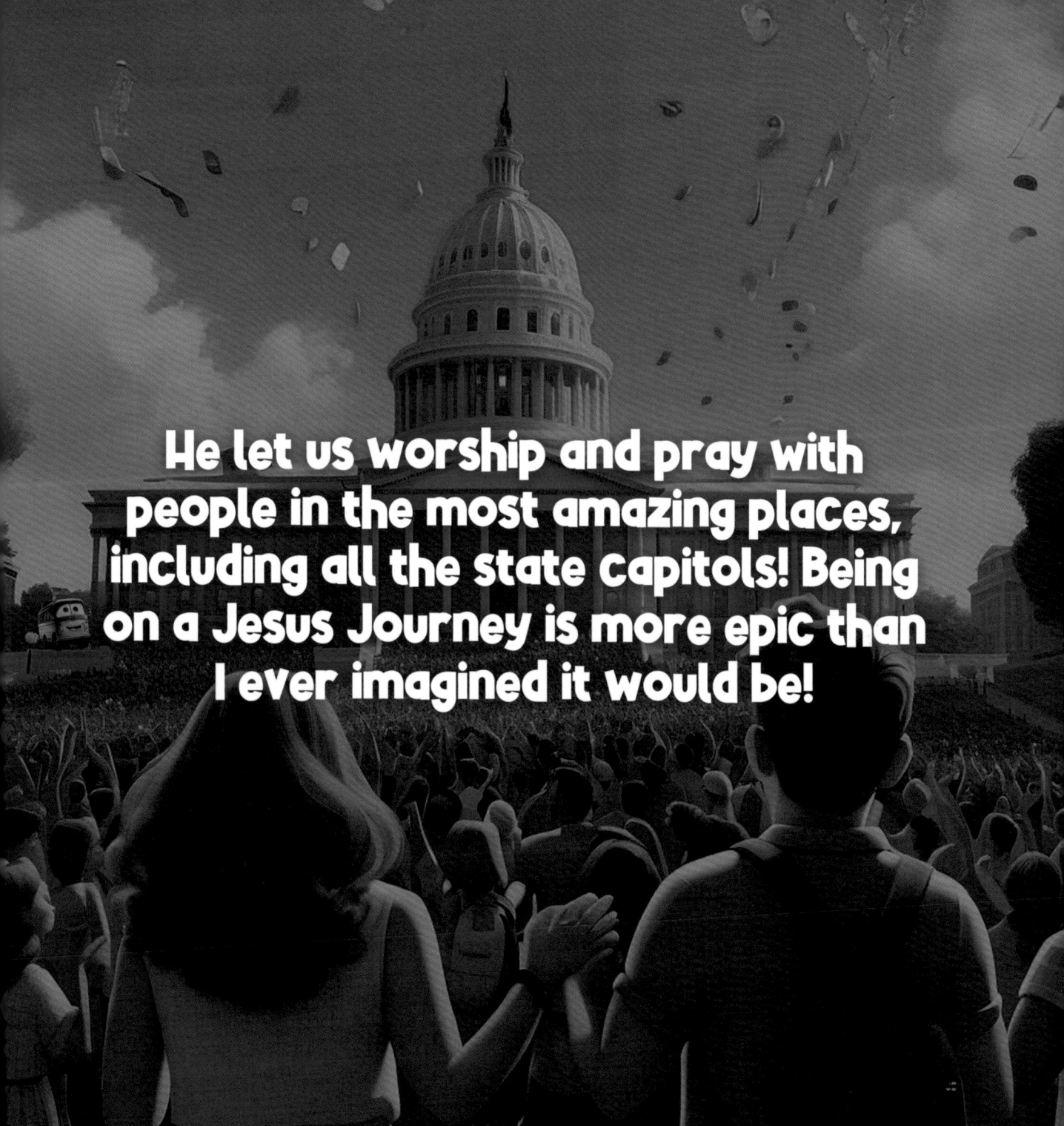

Just as we were wrapping up our time in the Midwest to head to the East Coast, we found out that our friends in Vermont were in trouble! There was a MASSIVE flood!

God's timing is always perfect. It was His plan for us to go there right when our friends needed help.

OH, NO!

On our way, while I was driving, another car wasn't looking at the road and ran right into me! It was so, so scary, and I ended up with a broken door.

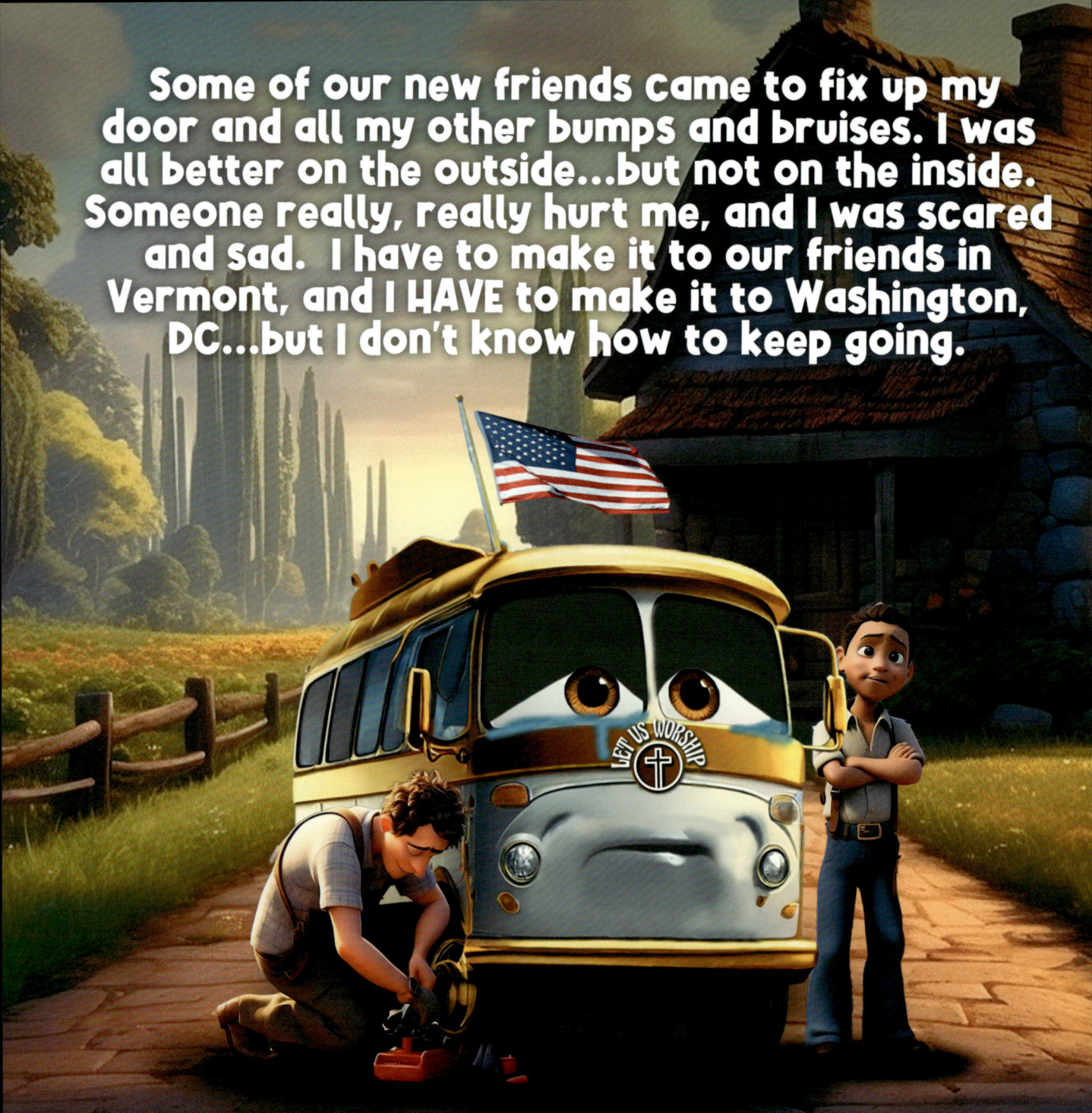

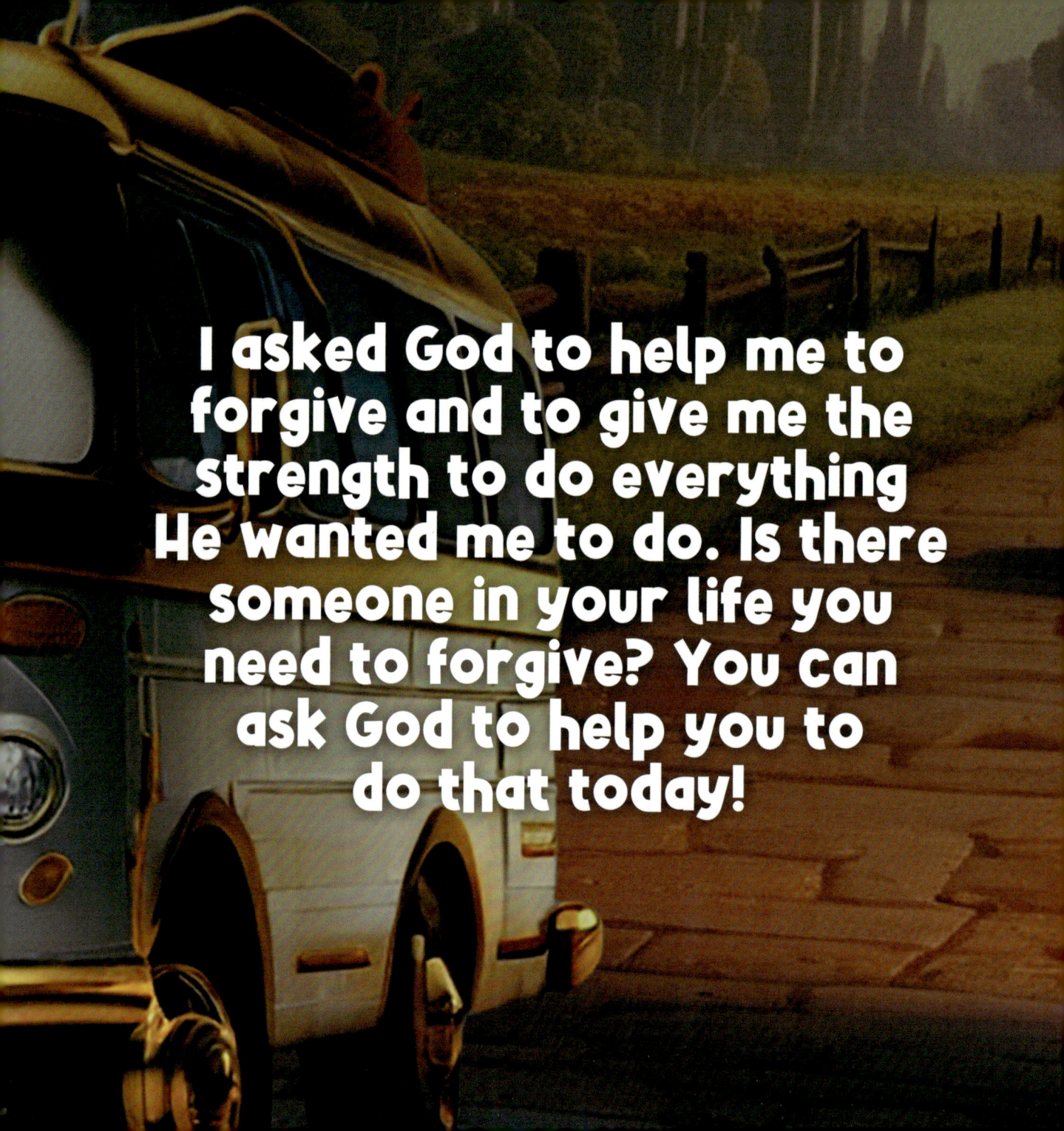

We were finally headed to Vermont, but not before every single one of my compartments was filled up with donated food and supplies to give away.

UH, OH! There's a HUMONGOUS storm cloud covering the entire city. But we know that if we pray, God can move the storm.

Did you know...?

When you give your life to Jesus, He takes you on a life-long adventure! Sometimes it can be really tough and sometimes it's really amazing, but the best part is that Jesus is always with you and always has a great plan. Do you want to give your life to Jesus and be on His adventure forever? You can start with this prayer:

Dear Heavenly Father,

I know that I'm not perfect and that I sin every single day. Thank you for sending Jesus to die on the cross for my sins. I want to live my life YOUR way and not my way. I want to go on YOUR adventure! Please come into my heart, and be my Best Friend and the Lord of my life. Fill me with the Holy Spirit, and help me to live for you. I now know who I am: I am loved, I am chosen, and I am a child of God.

In Jesus' Name,
Amen

LET US WORSHIP
KINGDOM TO THE CAPITOL TOUR

When God told Sean Feucht to worship in every capitol city, in all 50 states of America, he knew it would be very hard! Sean knew that he had to be obedient to Jesus, no matter what. God loves America so much and wants its leaders to know His love for them. God wants America to be righteous and to obey His laws.

Sean and his amazing team traveled to every state capitol and worshipped Jesus with tens of thousands of other Christians. This is only the beginning of Revival in America!

For more information, for more resources for children and teens, or to join us at an event near you, visit Seanfeucht.com or scan the QR code above.